MICHAEL FOREMAN

Grandfather's Pencil
AND THE ROOM OF STORIES

Library of Congress Cataloging-in-Publication Data available upon request.

ISBN 0-15-200061-5

A B C D E

HARCOURT BRACE & COMPANY
San Diego   New York   London
Printed and bound in Italy

THE BOY finished the letter to his father.

He put down his pencil and climbed into bed.

He kissed his mother goodnight.
　　All was quiet. The house slept in the moonlight.
The boy dreamed in his bed. The pencil lay on
the paper.

Then there was a scratchy, scribbly sound. The pencil was writing.

"I remember," wrote the pencil. "I remember when I first came to this house. I was in a box with friends. We were all different colors. We were a present for the boy."

"I remember the shop where we were bought. The shelves were full of bottles of ink and boxes of paints lined up in sets like soldiers."

"And paper—so many kinds of paper—smooth, rough thick, thin. Papers from all over the world. Oh, the stories they told, in the night, in the dark!"

"I remember the forest where we lived before we were pencils. I was part of a very tall tree. In my dreams I still feel the sway of the treetop in the wind."

In the boy's room a slight breeze ruffled the paper.

Then the pencil wrote as the paper told its tale. . . .

"I also remember when the men came and many trees were cut down. I remember the dragging of the logs and the thrilling journey down the river," said the paper.

"I remember that journey," the table joined in. "Harum-
scarum over the rapids, swinging round the bends. I also
remember the hook and chains and screaming saw blades."

"And then the quiet of the workshop and the loving hands that made me what I am today."

All was quiet in the room while the pencil wrote the table's tale.

"Do you remember those early days in the forest?" squeaked the door as it slowly opened. "Our hopes and dreams? Would we stay safe in the forest or travel the world? We have come a long way, but the boy has yet far to go."

The boy stirred in his bed. A pool of moonlight lay on the floorboards of the room.

"We have come farther than any of you," croaked the floorboards. "Long before this house was built we were part of a great ship with cream sails and a black flag."

"We lived on tar and salt and loved every pitching, rolling minute of the wind in the rigging and the swish of the sea. Oh, to feel such a wind again!"

"You will!" cried the old wooden window as it flew open.
The night wind whirled madly into the room.

The boy sat up, his eyes wild with excitement. The door danced on its hinges, the pencil rolled off the table and dropped into the pool of moonlight, and the paper flew out the window.

Out, over, and beyond the city, tumbling and swooping in the sky until it was caught and held in the topmost branches of a tree in the forest.

And these tales of the pencil, the paper, the door,
and the floorboards were torn by the wind.

Birds wove the tattered tales
into their nests and sang the stories
to their young. All the animals of the
forest listened, and so the stories
spread from the highest leaf to the
deepest root. The stories had come
home to the forest.

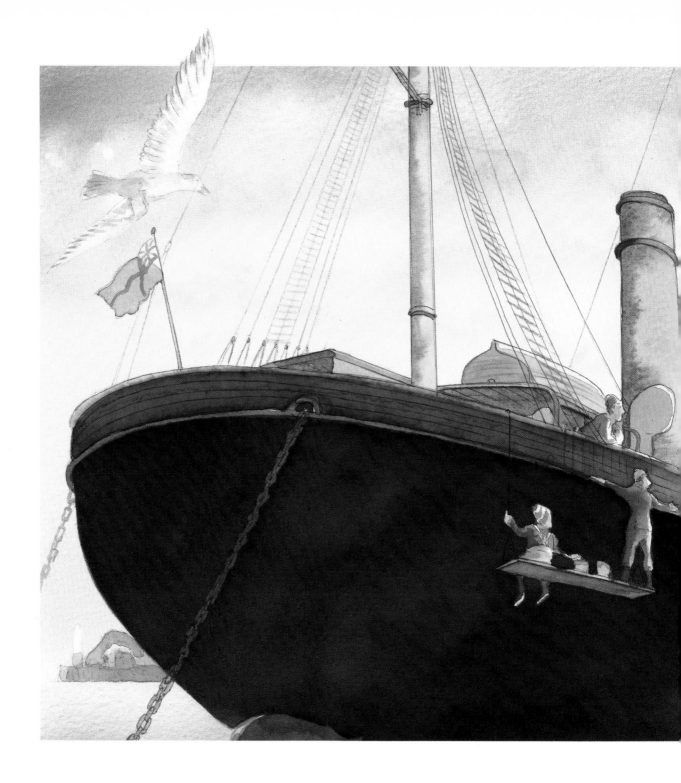

And the boy? The boy who had far to go?

He grew up and sailed the oceans of the world.

When he grew too old to sail, he lived in a
wooden house by the sea and told his stories to his
grandson, Jack. At night he slept in a sea of dreams.

Then, one day, he told Jack of the night, long,
long ago, when his boyhood room had filled with
the night wind, and the door danced and a pencil
stood on its point before it plunged into a pool of
moonlight and disappeared.

"It was in your room, Jack. In your house in
the city."

When Jack got back to the city, he rushed straight to his room.

He lay on the floor and peered through the cracks
between the old boards. He couldn't see anything. It was
pitch black.

Jack straightened a wire coat hanger, then lowered and raised it between the boards. He found several things of his own that he had lost and half forgotten.

Finally, he hooked out an old pencil!

He tried it on his notepad. It made a lovely, soft line. Jack wrote a "thank you for a lovely holiday" letter to his grandfather and added: "P.S. I have found the pencil!"

His mother came and kissed him goodnight, and he went to sleep.

The pencil lay on the paper. All was quiet.

Scritch, scratch. The pencil began to write. . . .

"For many years I have lain in the dark. My companions have been a bent pin, an old gold coin, and a whalebone button. Oh, the tales they told! The whale button remembered when it was part of a great whale and . . .

But that is another story.